Dear Parent:

Congratulations! Your child is taking the first steps on an exciting journey. The destination? Independent reading!

STEP INTO READING® will help your child get there. The program offers five steps to reading success. Each step includes fun stories and colorful art. There are also Step into Reading Sticker Books, Step into Reading Math Readers, Step into Reading Write-In Readers, Step into Reading Phonics Readers, and Step into Reading Phonics First Steps! Boxed Sets—a complete literacy program with something for every child.

Learning to Read, Step by Step!

Ready to Read Preschool–Kindergarten
• big type and easy words • rhyme and rhythm • picture clues
For children who know the alphabet and are eager to begin reading.

Reading with Help Preschool–Grade 1
• basic vocabulary • short sentences • simple stories
For children who recognize familiar words and sound out new words with help.

Reading on Your Own Grades 1–3
• engaging characters • easy-to-follow plots • popular topics
For children who are ready to read on their own.

Reading Paragraphs Grades 2–3
• challenging vocabulary • short paragraphs • exciting stories
For newly independent readers who read simple sentences with confidence.

Ready for Chapters Grades 2–4
• chapters • longer paragraphs • full-color art
For children who want to take the plunge into chapter books but still like colorful pictures.

STEP INTO READING® is designed to give every child a successful reading experience. The grade levels are only guides. Children can progress through the steps at their own speed, developing confidence in their reading, no matter what their grade.

Remember, a lifetime love of reading starts with a single step!

For school librarians everywhere
—S.L. & M.L.

Text copyright © 2006 by Sally Lucas.
Illustrations copyright © 2006 by Margeaux Lucas.

www.stepintoreading.com
www.randomhouse.com/kids

Educators and librarians, for a variety of teaching tools, visit us at
www.randomhouse.com/teachers

Library of Congress Cataloging-in-Publication Data
Lucas, Sally.
Dancing dinos go to school / by Sally Lucas ; illustrated by Margeaux Lucas. — 1st ed.
    p.   cm. — (Step into reading. Step 1 book)
SUMMARY: A surprised librarian and a young reader watch as dancing dinosaurs in a book leap
off the page and into the school, causing havoc in the classroom and on the playground.
ISBN 0-375-83241-6 (trade) — ISBN 0-375-93241-0 (lib. bdg.)
[1. Dinosaurs—Fiction. 2. Schools—Fiction. 3. Stories in rhyme.] I. Lucas, Margeaux, ill.
II. Title. III. Series.
PZ8.3.L966Das 2005   [E]—dc22   2005011572

Printed in the United States of America
20 19 18 17
First Edition

STEP INTO READING®

STEP 1

by Sally Lucas
illustrated by Margeaux Lucas

Random House 🏠 New York

Dinos dancing

in a book.

Dinos leaping,
look, look, look!

Dinos landing

on the floor.

Dinos dancing
more and more.

Dinos peeking

through the glass.

Dinos sneaking

into class.

Jiggling, wiggling

to and fro.

Wiping chalkboards

as they go.

Dinos reading ABC.

Dinos counting 1, 2, 3.

Dinos pasting

red and blue.

Dinos wasting

paint and glue.

Dinos taking

every snack.

Dinos putting
each one back.

Dinos running

out to play.

Dinos cheering

all the way.

Dinos jumping

hand in hand.

Dinos digging
in the sand.

Dinos soaring

on the swings.

Higher, higher—

School bell rings!

Stopping, dropping
very fast.

Chasing, racing

back at last.

Dinos leaping,

look, look, look.

Dinos dancing
in a book.